Little Rooster's DIAMOND BUTTON

Retold by

Margaret Read MacDonald

Illustrated by **Will Terry**

ALBERT WHITMAN & COMPANY, MORTON GROVE, ILLINOIS

For Julie . . . who loved Little Rooster's French cousin, Drakestail, so much that she hid the library book under her bed for four years!—M.R.M.

For Justine, Brookley, and Seth . . . best friends.—W.T.

Somewhere . . . someplace . . . across the seven seas . . . there lived a little old woman and her little pet rooster.

One day Little Rooster went to peck out something to eat.
He pecked and he pecked and . . . he pecked up a diamond button!

"Cock-a-doodle-doo! Cock-a-doodle-doo!

I'll take this home to my good mistress!
She likes diamond buttons!"

But here came the King with his servants.
The King wore such baggy trousers that he could hardly walk.

When the King saw the diamond button . . . he wanted it!
"Take that diamond button! Put it in my treasure chamber!"

Little Rooster flew right to the King's palace.
"Cock-a-doodle-doo! Cock-a-doodle-doo!
Give me back my diamond button!"

The King was MAD.
"Throw that Little Rooster into the well!
Get rid of him!"

They threw Little Rooster into a well.
But Little Rooster had a *magic* stomach!
"Come, my empty stomach. Come, my empty stomach.
Drink up all the water in the well!"
His magic stomach drank up all the water in the well!

Little Rooster flew right back to the King's palace and said,
"Cock-a-doodle-doo! Cock-a-doodle-doo!
Give me back my diamond button!"

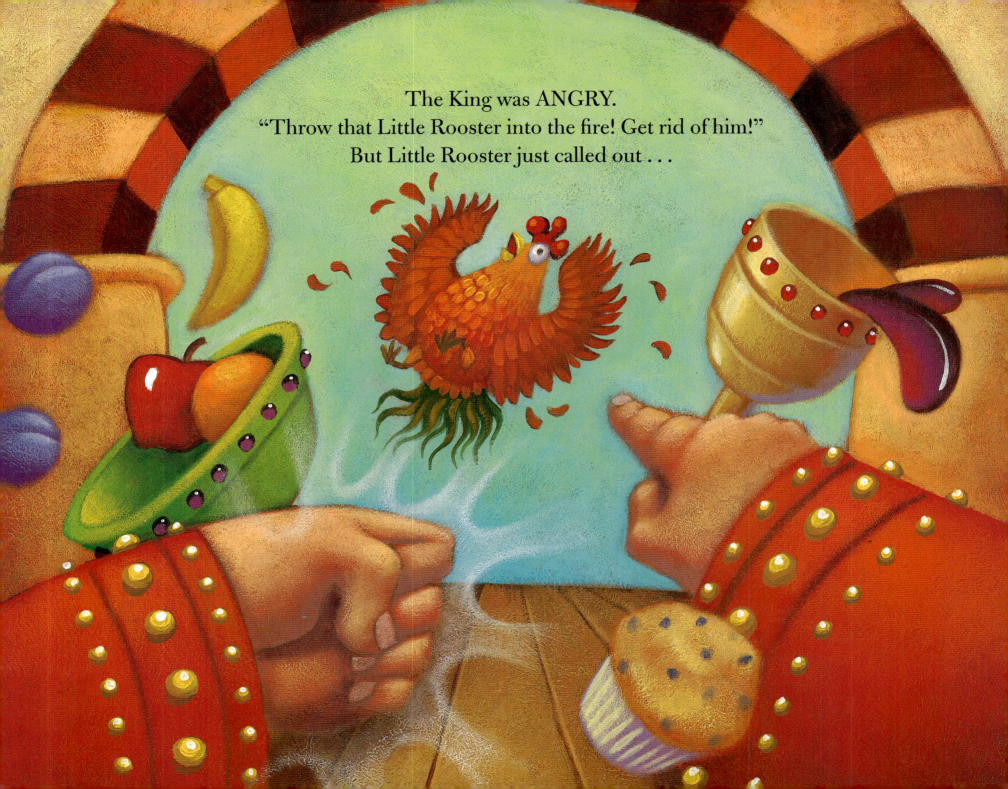

The King was ANGRY.
"Throw that Little Rooster into the fire! Get rid of him!"
But Little Rooster just called out . . .

"Come, my *full* stomach. Come, my *full* stomach.
Spit out all the water from the well *and put out the fire!*"

Little Rooster flew right back to the King's palace.
"Cock-a-doodle-doo! Cock-a-doodle-doo!
Give me back my diamond button!"
The King was FURIOUS!
"Throw that Little Rooster into a BEEHIVE!
Let the bees sting him!"
But . . .

"Come, my empty stomach.
Come, my empty stomach.
Eat up all the . . . BEES!"
His stomach ate up all the bees.
"Bzzzzzzz!"
But the bees could not sting his magic stomach.

Little Rooster flew right back to the King's palace.
"Cock-a-doodle-doo! Cock-a-doodle-doo!
Give me back my diamond button!"
The King was INFURIATED.

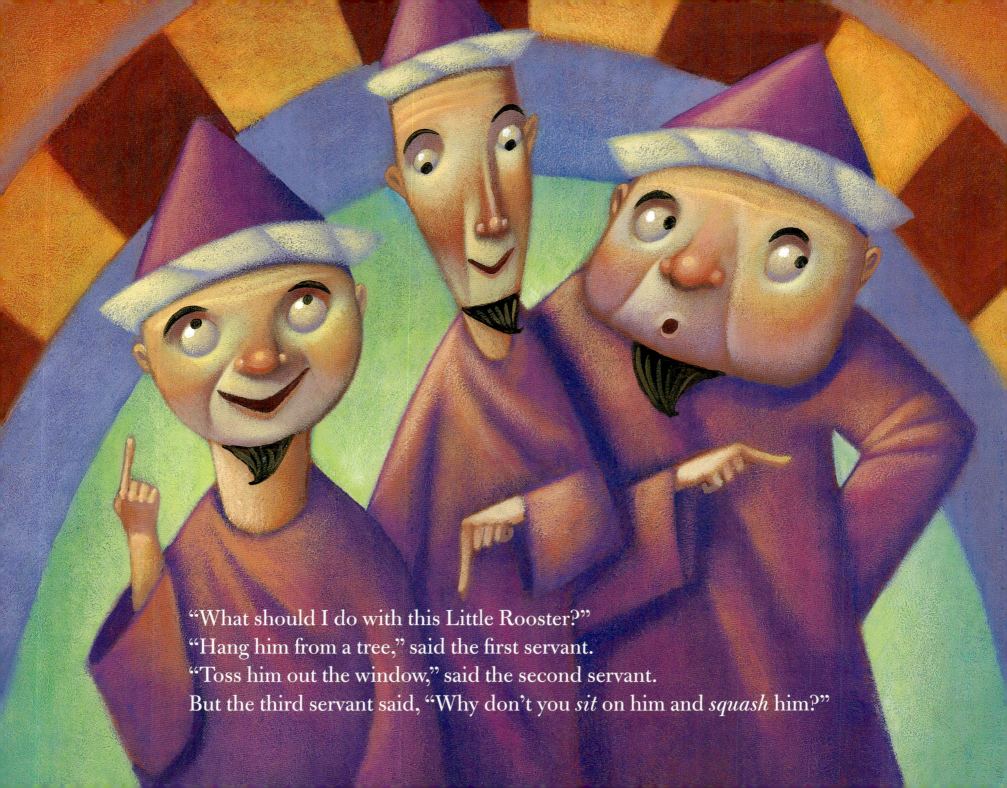

"What should I do with this Little Rooster?"
"Hang him from a tree," said the first servant.
"Toss him out the window," said the second servant.
But the third servant said, "Why don't you *sit* on him and *squash* him?"

"I like that idea!" said the King. "Drop him into my baggy pants.
I am going to SIT on him!"
So they dropped Little Rooster into the King's baggy pants.
And the King started to sit on him.

But Little Rooster called out,
"Come, my *full* stomach. Come, my *full* stomach.
Spit out all the *bees* . . . and let them *sting that King!*"

AY, AY, AY! Those bees did sting!
"Take that Little Rooster away!" cried the King.
"Let him *have* his old diamond button.
I never want to *see* him again!"

They took the Little Rooster to the King's treasure chamber.
"Take your diamond button and go along home!"

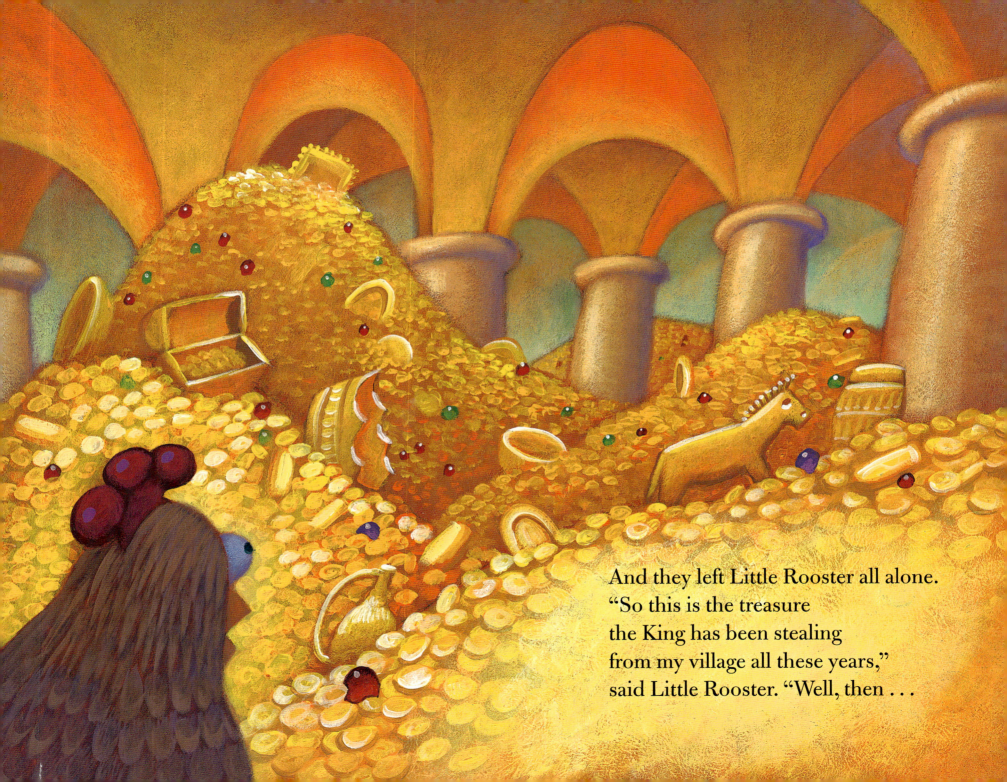

And they left Little Rooster all alone.
"So this is the treasure
the King has been stealing
from my village all these years,"
said Little Rooster. "Well, then . . .

"Come, my empty stomach. Come, my empty stomach.
Eat up all the treasure in the King's treasure chamber!"
His stomach ate up all the rubies . . . all the emeralds . . . all the
gold and silver . . . all the diamonds . . . and the diamond button, too!
Then he went along home.

"Cock-a-doodle-doo! Cock-a-doodle-doo!
Come, my *full* stomach. Come, my *full* stomach.
Spit out all the treasure!"

There was treasure enough for all the village.
And Little Rooster and his good mistress lived richly and happily ever after.

Note

This tale has long been a favorite of storytellers and has appeared in many picture books and folktale collections. My favorite telling was that in Kate Seredy's 1935 children's novel *The Good Master*. There, the Hungarian grandmother tells the story, and the villain is the Turkish sultan. For hundreds of years, Hungary had been under Turkish occupation, and the memory was still strong. Folklore Motif Z52, in which a bird swallows many helpful objects which rout the king, appears in stories from many countries, including India, Burma, Poland, and Russia. Well-known variants are the stories of Drakestail from France and Medio Pollito from Spain.

Library of Congress Cataloging-in-Publication Data

MacDonald, Margaret Read, 1940-   Little Rooster's diamond button/retold by Margaret Read MacDonald ; illustrated by Will Terry.

p. cm. Summary: A rooster with a magic stomach retrieves the diamond button which was stolen from him by a greedy king.

ISBN 13: 978-0-8075-4644-4 (hardcover) [1. Folklore—Hungary.] I. Terry, Will, 1966- , ill. II. Title.

PZ8.1.M15924Lit 2007 398.2—dc22 [E] 2006023979

The design is by Carol Gildar.

The illustrations were done in acrylic on paper.

For information about Albert Whitman & Company, please visit our web site at www.albertwhitman.com.